2-3
FIRST GRADE

DeLage, Ida
Whitchey Broom

DATE DUE

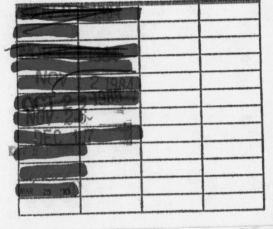

NOV 2 1984			
OCT 23 1985			
NOV 28			
DEC 17			
MAR 25 '90			

Tall Tales books bring to the primary reader stories filled with boisterous action, humor, and excitement. Some are based on folklore; others are pure fantasy.

All the books have colorful illustrations that capture to perfection the gay, carefree mood of the text.

Each author has created an imaginative, easy-to-read story designed to entice the reader into the magic realm of books.

The Witchy Broom

By Ida DeLage

Pictures by Walt Peaver

GARRARD PUBLISHING COMPANY
CHAMPAIGN, ILLINOIS

Copyright © 1969 by Ida DeLage
All rights reserved. Manufactured in the U.S.A.
Standard Book Number 8116-4054-X
Library of Congress Catalog Card Number: 69-10373

The Witchy Broom

The moon was round,
the leaves were brown.
An old witch went
creeping . . . creeping
through the woods.
She was gathering fagots
to make her fire.

When her basket was full
the old witch hopped
upon her broom.
Swish — swish. She flew
back to her cave.
She had to hurry
and cook her magic brew.

It was almost Halloween.
"Figgoty faggoty
Fire burn hot.
Snap and crackle
Beneath my pot,"
chanted the old witch.

Into her fire
the old witch threw
some twigs
to make it burn,
some pine cones
to make it snap,
some rotten eggshells
to make it crackle,
2 crow's feathers
to make the sparks fly,
3 hairs from a skunk's tail
to make it smell nice.
She fanned it
with her old black hat.

The fire began
to dance and leap.
"Eee-hee-hee,"
cackled the old witch.
"Now my brew
will steam and stew."

9

Then . . .

all of a sudden,

"Eee-eek!"

shrieked the old witch.

"My broom!

My broom is on fire!"

Sure enough!
The broom had fallen
into the fire.
It was crackling and burning
along with the twigs.
The old witch snatched it
out of the fire.
But it was too late.
There was nothing left
but the handle!

The old witch muttered
and she sputtered.
She pulled her hair
and waggled her chin.
She moaned
and she groaned.
Oh, what bad luck!
A witch without a broom
on Halloween,
is no good at all.
She had to fix her broom.
The old witch
took her broom handle
and hobbled off.

Down the hill she went
and across the valley.
It was a long way
to the big black swamp
where the brown rushes grew.
The stones hurt her feet
and her shoes pinched her toes.
Oh how she wished
she could ride her broom!
Just as she was creeping by
the old farmer's house,
the old witch stopped.
There, on the back porch,
was a brand new broom!

"Eee-ee! How lovely!
Just what I need!"
cackled the old witch.
She hobbled over to the porch
and took the new broom.

14

"Oh you pretty little pet,"
she said.
"Your tail is short
but you will do.
You will do."
Then, to make it magic
so it could fly,
the old witch chanted
a magic spell over it.

"Broom broom
Zip and zoom.
Ride the winds
Up to the moon."

The old witch hopped on
the new magic broom.
Swish! It flew like a bird.
In no time at all
the old witch came to
the big black swamp.
She picked some brown rushes.
Soon she made her old broom
as good as new.
The old witch quickly
got upon her mended broom.
Now . . . witches cast spells
and haunt houses,
but they never, never steal.

So on the way back to her cave
the witch put the new broom
on the farmer's porch again.
But . . .
she forgot to take the magic
out of it!

The next morning
the farmer's wife came out
to sweep off the back porch.
She picked up her new broom.
Swish! There she was
up in the apple tree!

The old farmer came by.
"Hey there, Ma," he called.
"What are you doing
up there in the apple tree?"

"You'll never guess, Pa,
if you guess all day,"
said his wife.
"That broom can fly!
I can't get down."
The old farmer was a little deaf.
He thought she said,
"I'll bake you a pie
so nice and brown."
"Ho, ho!" laughed the farmer.
"That's the best news
I've heard today."
And off he went
to milk the cows.

After a while
the farmer came back
for his dinner.
"Say, Ma," he called.
"Are you still picking apples?"
"No, you deaf old man,"
hollered his wife.
"I'm not picking apples.
I told you
I flew up here on my broom."
"Ho ho," laughed the farmer.
"That's a good joke!"
Then he saw the broom.
He picked it up.

ZOOM! The farmer flew
like a rocket
to the top of the silo!
"By gollys, Ma,
you're right,"
hollered the old farmer.
"This broom CAN fly!"

The farmer climbed down
from the silo.
He got a ladder
and helped his wife
get down from the apple tree.
"There's something funny
going on around here,"
said the farmer.
"You're right,"
said the wife.
"And I know what.
A witch has been around.
This broom is a
WITCHY broom!"

"You don't say!"
declared the farmer.
"A WITCHY broom?
Hmm-mm.
I wonder if I can fly it
and steer it
where I want to go."

25

The farmer hopped on
the witchy broom.
Swish! Off it flew.
The farmer steered it
all around the apple tree.

"Say! This is great!"
shouted the smart old farmer.
"This witchy broom can do
a lot of work for me."

The farmer got his spray gun.
He hopped on the witchy broom.
Swish — swish — swish.
He sprayed his apple tree.

Then he got
his can of yellow paint.
Swish — swish — swish.
He painted his barn.

"Land sakes alive, Pa,"
said the farmer's wife.
"It looks like fun
to ride that broom.
I do believe I'll try
a little spin around."
So the farmer's wife
hopped on the witchy broom.

Swish — she flew
all around the house.
Then she flew over the garden
to look at her flowers
and down to the brook
to see the ducks.
"Whee-ee!" she said.
"This is fun!"

The old black crow
was flying over the cornfield.
He dropped the corn
he had in his beak.
"Caw — caw — caw," he said.
He was 100 years old.
Never in his life
had he seen such a sight!

The cows stopped
chewing their cuds.
The chickens stopped
pulling up worms.
The pigs stopped
rolling in the mud.
They wondered,
"What in the world
is that?"

The moon came up
very early that night.
The old farmer and his wife
went to bed.
They forgot it was Halloween!
Some boys came sneaking along.
They were going to play
some tricks on the old farmer.
"Let's put the goat
on the barn roof," said Tom.
"Let's roll the wagon
down the hill," said Dick.
"Let's chase the horse
down the road," said Butch.

Just then the farmer's wife
heard some noise.

She peeked out the window.
She saw the boys
creeping around.
"Ah ha!" she said.
"Those boys are up to no good.
I'll play a trick on them."
So the farmer's wife put on
her old black dress
and the farmer's straw hat.
Then . . .
she hopped on the witchy broom
and flew right over
the boys' heads.
"Ooo-oo-oo," she said.

The boys looked up.
"Jeepers! A witch!"
they said.
They ran across the meadow.
"Creepers!" they said.
"Another witch!"
They jumped into the haystack
and hid.

Sure enough!
Who should it be
but the real old witch.
She was flying along
with her jug of brew
under her arm.
She was going to cast
some spells around the farm.

"Tee-hee-hee,"
cackled the old witch.
"I guess I scared those boys
half to death."
Suddenly, the old witch
almost bumped into someone.
"Eee-eek,"
shrieked the witch.
Oh! Was she angry!
How dare another witch
come here.
Then she saw
it was the farmer's wife
on the witchy broom.

"Heh, heh, heh.
I'll fix her," said the witch.
"I'm the only one
who flies around here!"
 "Snip sneep
 Fall in a heap.
 Once you flew
 But now you sweep,"
chanted the old witch.

Instantly,
all the magic left
the new witchy broom.
PLOP!
There was the farmer's wife
right in the middle
of the haystack!

"Wow!" hollered the boys.
"The old witch is after us!
Run for your life!"
The boys ran so fast
they jumped over the fence
with one leap
and beat the dog home.

The old witch laughed so hard
she flew upside down.
All of her brew
leaked out of her jug.
She had to go back to her cave
and cook some more.

The farmer's wife jumped
off the haystack.
She grabbed her broom
and said,
"Fly away witchy broom
with a leap, leap, leap."
But all that broom
could ever do again
was sweep, sweep, sweep.

Lift your eyes
to the sky
my dears,
Though your feet
be on the ground.
Where the moon is hung
The stars are flung
And strange things
fly around.